The Bib

by Susan Hartley • illustrated by Anita DuFalla

Pam has the pan.

Bob has a bib for Tam.

Bob has a bib for Sam.

Tam bit the cob.

The cob is hot for Tam.

Bob can fan the cob.

Fan the cob for Tam, Bob.

Tim can see the cob.

Tim has no cob.
Tim has the bat.
Tim bit the bat.